To Kristen Bennett
from aunt Rose
1990

Text copyright © 1975 Intercontinental Book Productions assigned to Victoria House Publishing Limited
Artwork copyright © 1982 Purnell Publishers Limited
Artwork copyright © Macdonald & Co (Publishers) Ltd 1988
First published 1982 by Purnell Books
Reprinted 1988 by Macdonald & Co (Publishers) Ltd under the Black Cat imprint

Macdonald & Co (Publishers) Ltd
3rd Floor
Greater London House
Hampstead Road
London NW1 7QX

a member of Maxwell Pergamon Publishing Corporation plc

ISBN 0-7481-0096-2

Printed in GDR

The story in this book is derived from *Heidi* by Johanna Spyri

Heidi

Johanna Spyri

BLACK CAT

Retold by Jane Carruth

Heidi's New Home

WHAT A strange pair they made as they struggled up the steep mountainside! The tall strong-looking woman was obviously in a great hurry as she pulled after her a child who couldn't be more than five years old.

"Come on, Heidi," she shouted impatiently every now and then. "Hurry up."

Poor Heidi! It was June and the sun was shining brightly, but her aunt Dete had dressed her as if it was deepest winter. She was wearing at least three dresses, one on top of the other, and over these a heavy red woollen shawl was wrapped round her shoulders. It was quite impossible to tell whether she was thin or fat under all her clothes.

They had left the little Swiss town of Maienfeld at the foot of the mountain quite an hour ago and now they were climbing, climbing to the wooden shack where Alm-Uncle lived with his two goats.

"Why is he called Alm-Uncle?" Heidi asked Dete, who was striding on ahead.

"Because he has chosen to live on this mountain which is called the Alm," said Dete. "We always called him 'uncle' because he was distantly related to my mother."

"Is he my uncle too?" Heidi wanted to know next.

"No," said Dete sharply, "he is your grandfather. His son was your father."

"I don't remember my father or my mother," said Heidi sadly.

Dete stopped to give Heidi a rest. "Of course you don't," she said a little more kindly. "They died when you were a baby. Then my mother took care of you. And now she's dead, too."

"Is that why you are taking me to Grandfather?" Heidi asked. And Dete nodded. "He's got to take his turn at looking after you," she said quickly, and before Heidi could ask any more questions, she started up the mountainside again.

When they were half way up Dete met an old friend of hers, called Barbel. Barbel lived in the village of Dorfli, a hamlet built on the side of the Alm. She was very surprised to see Dete and Heidi.

"You're not taking that poor child to live with Alm-Uncle," she whispered when Dete told her the purpose of their visit. "You must be out of your mind, Dete! You can't do such a thing. The old man is so surly and bad-tempered, nobody dares speak to him. He never comes down to the village. I really don't think he has a friend in the world."

"It can't be helped," said Dete, looking a little bit uncomfortable. "I've been offered a good job away from home, and I mean to take it. Somebody has to look after the child and Alm-Uncle must be the one to do it. There's no one else I can ask, after all."

Barbel looked round to see if Heidi was listening, but the little girl had found a friend. She was talking to Peter, the goatherd. He was a young boy, not much older than Heidi, who lived with his mother and his blind grandmother in a tumbledown hut in the hamlet. Every day he took the goats up the mountain to find fresh green grass and now he and Heidi were laughing together as they ran after the friendly goats.

Dete called sharply to her and Heidi ran back, a little out of breath, but her cheeks now rosy and her eyes shining. Together they began to climb again.

After a few steps Dete turned round and saw that Peter was standing still, staring at them, with a half-smile on his face. "If you have nothing better to do," she said sharply, "you can carry this bundle for me to Alm-Uncle's place." And she held out a parcel to the shabbily dressed, bare-footed boy.

Peter shook his head but when he saw that Dete had taken a coin from her bag, he snatched the bundle and ran off, taking the shortest and steepest path up the mountain.

It was nearly another hour's climb before Heidi saw the wooden hut which was to be her home. It stood on a flat piece of rock, at the mercy of the winds, but where every ray of the sun could rest upon it. From its perch it had a marvellous view of the valley below. Behind the hut stood three old fir trees, with long, thick branches, and beyond them the mountain continued to climb upwards, its lower slopes covered with bright green grass and beautiful wild flowers.

Heidi ran forward when she saw the hut. She reached the door before Dete and there, sitting on a roughly made wooden bench, sat a rather fierce-looking old man. 'That must be my grandfather,' thought Heidi, so she walked up to him, put out her hand and said, "Good-evening, Grandfather."

The old man looked at her steadily from under his thick bushy eyebrows but Heidi met his gaze without flinching.

At last Dete arrived, quite out of breath. "Good-day to you, Uncle," she said. "I have brought you Tobias's child. You've not seen her since your son died but she is your grand-daughter and it's up to you to take care of her." She spoke very quickly as if she was afraid of being interrupted.

"And what if she will not stay with me?" asked the old man gruffly.

"That's your business," said Dete, as she became more confident. "I've done my duty by her for four years, looking after her as best I could and I can tell you it hasn't always been convenient. Now you must take your turn."

Then she turned and half ran down the mountainside before the old man could say anything to stop her. She hadn't even said goodbye to Heidi.

Heidi and her Grandfather

SO HEIDI'S new life with her grandfather began. From the very first, she loved the silent old man with his long grey whiskers and rough hands. And oh, how she loved the mountains and the fir trees and the little hut and the two pretty goats.

"What are they called, Grandfather?" she asked, on the second day.

The old man took the pipe out of his mouth. "The white one is called Little Swan and the brown one is called Little Bear," he told her, hiding a smile, when he saw her sparkling eyes. It was the first time he had smiled for a long time.

"I won't need any of my stuffy dresses any more," Heidi told him next. "Just the old comfortable one. From now on I mean to run with the goats all over the mountain."

In Heidi's eyes her life with the old man was perfect and she had all she wanted in the world. Her grandfather had made her the most comfortable bed she had ever slept in, in the hay-loft. Each evening she climbed up the little ladder and fell asleep looking at the stars twinkling in the sky.

Her very own stool was specially made for her by her grandfather too: it was just a little circle of wood with three holes, into which he had fixed three long, round sticks. Every morning she sat on her three-legged stool at the bare wooden table. Her grandfather gave her a bowl filled with sweet goat's milk and bread with toasted cheese. Heidi thought it was all delicious.

She soon learnt that everything in the hut had its proper place and as she ran from cupboard to table and reached up to the shelves, the old man would follow her with his eyes and then smile quietly to himself.

Heidi's cheeks grew rosier each day with all the fresh air and good food she was having. In the mornings when the sun's rays turned everything to gold, she loved nothing more than to run with Peter as he took the villagers' goats up the mountain. When he reached Alm-Uncle's hut he would collect Little Swan and Little Bear so they could graze with the other goats where the grass was green and lush.

And Heidi would go too. The flowers, the bright patches of red primroses and the blue gentian delighted her and she would laugh and shout as she ran bare-footed after Peter, her curls tossed by the wind.

Peter liked having her with him. He had often been lonely before, always being on his own, and her bright company helped to pass the time. Also, Alm-Uncle always gave Heidi enough fresh bread and cheese for the two of them. The goats seemed better behaved too — Heidi had only to call and even the naughtiest of them would come running to her.

Heidi loved the goats, but the prettiest of them all were Little Swan and Little Bear.

"That's because Alm-Uncle always brushes them down and washes them and gives them salt," Peter told her. "And he has the nicest shed for them, where they are warm and cozy and out of the wind."

Each night, Heidi would sit quietly with her grandfather telling him about her wonderful day, and the old man sucked at his pipe and listened. Then he would tell her how, each night, the sun said good-night to the mountain which explained why it looked as if it were on fire.

Soon autumn came and the winds blew round the little hut. It could be dangerous on the mountain now, so Heidi's grandfather told her she must stay at home.

Heidi listened to the music coming from the three old fir trees as they sighed and swished in the wind. She was content to spend the hours with her grandfather.

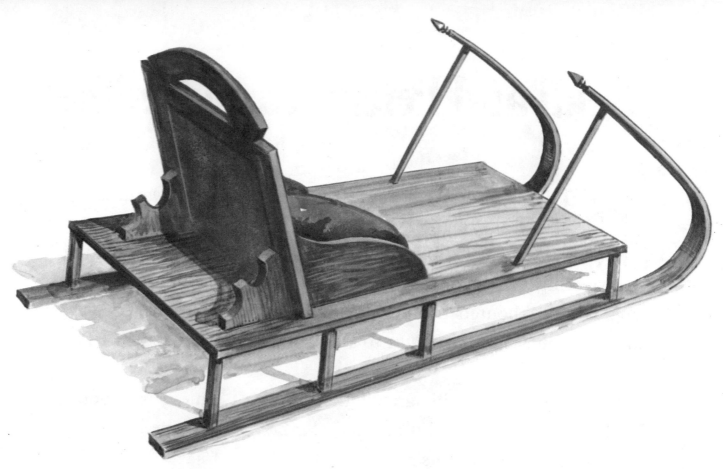

Peter wasn't so happy now that she could no longer go with him, so instead he would stop at the hut for a while and talk to her. He told her about his grandmother and how old and frail she was. And how hard it was for his mother to take care of her for they had hardly any money.

One morning, Heidi awoke to find the whole world covered with a thick mantle of gleaming snow. She looked at it in dismay.

"Today I wanted to go down the mountain and visit Peter's grandmother," she said, as she drank her milk.

"And so you shall," said her grandfather. "But not until this afternoon."

Then he disappeared outside and all morning Heidi could hear the sound of sawing and hammering. When he came back indoors, he told her to run to the door and look out. There, resting on top of the snow, stood a wonderful hand-sleigh.

"That is your snow carriage, child," he said. "Together we will go down the mountain on it."

Heidi and Peter's Grandmother

THAT same afternoon, Heidi, wrapped up in a warm sack, was lifted on to the sleigh by her grandfather. Then he got in beside her, and before Heidi knew what was happening he was steering the sleigh down the mountain with a long pole. Heidi laughed and shouted her delight as they raced over the crisp white snow. When at last they came to a standstill, they were outside Peter's hut.

"Here we are," said her grandfather. "I won't come in with you. But I will wait at home until it grows dark, then I will come to fetch you. You must set out at the same time."

When Heidi stepped into the tiny room it seemed very bare and dark. As her eyes got used to the gloom she saw an old woman, very thin and bent, sitting in one corner at a spinning wheel.

"Good-day, Grandmother," she said, going over to her. "I have come at last to see you."

Heidi held out her hand and the old woman groped for it. When she found Heidi's outstretched hand, she held it for a long moment. There was something about Heidi's bright, friendly voice that made the old lady long for her sight so that she could see this child who had come down the mountain to visit her.

In a few moments, Heidi was telling her about her wonderful new home, her kind grandfather and the pretty goats.

"One day you shall see them for yourself," she promised.

The old woman shook her head. "I cannot see," she said. "I am quite blind."

Heidi's loving heart was so stricken when she realized that the old lady could see nothing of the beautiful world around, that she began to sob. Only Peter's sudden appearance put a stop to her crying. Then Brigitta, Peter's mother, said, "Don't be too upset, Heidi. The old lady is happier than she has been for a long time, just talking to you."

"I will come again," said Heidi. "I will come as often as I can. But now it's growing dark and I must set out for home."

Heidi had barely left the shabby little hut when she saw her grandfather striding down the mountain towards her. Quickly he wrapped her up in the warm sack he was carrying and, lifting her into his arms, he strode off up the mountain.

When they were safely home and Heidi had drunk her milk, she said, "Grandfather, we must go down again tomorrow. You must take your hammer and nails with you for when I sat with the old lady, I heard the wind whistling through the broken shutters. It is very cold inside, not at all like our warm and snug home."

Heidi looked at her grandfather with such trust that he smiled. "Very well," he said. "I will put a stop to the whistling wind and the rattles. Yes, yes, we shall go again tomorrow."

Although Alm-Uncle could never be persuaded to enter the hut, he made it secure from the outside so that the wind no longer blew indoors.

The old lady was forever blessing Heidi for the joy she had brought into her life.

"I love that child as if she were my own grand-daughter," she would say to Brigitta. "And I don't believe what they say about her grandfather in the village. How could he make a gentle child like Heidi happy if he were as surly and bad-tempered as they say he is! And look how kind he has been in making our little home cozy for me."

"Maybe," said Brigitta, "but the villagers still say he is a terrible old man and will have nothing to do with him when he goes for his bread. We'll just have to wait and see."

All through the winter, Heidi visited Peter's grandmother and the old lady welcomed her as if she were an angel sent from heaven. Sitting listening to Heidi's bright chatter, the time passed so quickly that the old lady was happier than she had been for years.

Then one day, the snow began to melt. Winter was nearly over. When Heidi saw the first flowers and heard the gentle swishing of the fir trees, she knew that Spring had really come again.

She was so happy that the seasons followed each other on wings. She had been on the mountain for three years, the happiest in her life, when one fateful day everything changed.

The Surprise Visitor

HEIDI WAS helping her grandfather to clear away the bowls one morning, shortly after her eighth birthday, when a visitor came to the hut. It was Dete, in a fine feathered hat and smart silken gown and wrap.

Dete wrinkled her nose with distaste as she looked around her. Then she said briskly, "I've come for you, Heidi!" And turning to the old man, she went on, "I know what a nuisance the child must have been. Well, now I've found a home for her. She can live with a rich family in Frankfurt and be companion to a sick, ailing girl, the daughter of the house. It will be good for her to live among civilized people and I assure you she will have everything she wants."

Heidi ran to her grandfather, clinging to him and the old man shouted, "Be off with you!" But Dete stood her ground. "I have more right over her than you do," she shouted back. "And besides, she is now eight years old but she has learnt nothing as you refuse to send her to school. Nor do you take her to church. What future does the child have here?"

"I'm not coming," said Heidi. "I don't want to leave."

"Come now," said Dete. "Get your clothes together. I suppose you'll have to wear that shabby old straw hat, but never mind, you'll soon have new clothes."

"No!" said Heidi. Suddenly her grandfather turned to Dete and said, "Go now, and I never want to see you again." And with that he pushed Heidi away and strode out of the hut.

"You see!" said Dete. "He doesn't really want you here." Then she began to persuade Heidi. "If you come with me for a short visit now, you will be able to get your grandfather a lovely present. Think of that! And it will be all the more fun when you come back."

The Journey

DETE BEGAN to bundle up a few clothes. She put the old straw hat on Heidi's head and took a firm grasp of her hand. "Come along!" she said. "Why, you are as obstinate as the goats!"

There was no sign of her beloved grandfather and, with a heavy heart, Heidi allowed herself to be pulled along, down the mountain.

She begged to go in and say goodbye to the blind old grandmother, who, having heard that Heidi was going, was standing at the door imploring Dete not to take her away. But Dete held on to the child, afraid that if she let her go now, she would never come with her.

They stayed the night in Maienfeld, Dete keeping a watchful eye over

Heidi. There, early the next morning they boarded a train for Frankfurt.

At last they arrived at the tall grey house, in the middle of the busy, unfriendly town. Heidi looked pale and wan and deeply unhappy, but Dete took no notice as she dragged her up the steps and rang the bell.

A maid opened the door and took them both up a long staircase to the housekeeper's room. Fraulein Rottenmeier, the housekeeper, was a tall disapproving lady, and she took an instant dislike to Heidi in her ragged clothes and shabby straw hat. This was not at all the sort of person she had in mind to be a companion to the young lady of the house!

"This is the girl," said Dete quickly. "I assure you she is very bright and friendly and will make an excellent companion for your master's invalid daughter."

Then, as if afraid that Heidi would not be accepted, she excused herself and hurried from the room.

'I don't think you will be at all suitable," said the housekeeper looking down her nose at Heidi. "You look much too young for one thing, but Clara has been looking forward to a companion so you had better come and meet her."

Clara, with her gentle blue eyes and pale thin face, liked Heidi at once. Heidi's heart went out to her and soon the two were chattering together like old friends.

"How I wish I could run and jump like you," Clara sighed, after she

had heard about the mountain and the goats. "But I can't even walk and I have to stay in this wheelchair. When my father is at home he takes me out, but he is usually away."

"I'll make you better," said Heidi confidently. "But it mustn't take too long, for my grandfather is waiting for me. And then there's Peter and the grandmother. She is blind but perhaps if she had nice things to eat, she would grow stronger."

Heidi opened her eyes and stared round the big room in bewilderment on her first morning in Frankfurt. Where was she? She thought she could still smell the sweet hay in her cozy loft. But this was not the loft. It was a great big room with a high ceiling. And she was lying in a high, white bed with crisp starched sheets.

Then she remembered where she was and jumped out of bed. She felt like a trapped animal as she stared out of the window at the tall grey buildings. All she longed for was the soft green grass of her mountain, the blue sky and the music of the fir trees in the wind.

That morning at breakfast, a tall young servant, called Sebastian, wheeled Clara up to the table where Heidi was already seated. Heidi's eyes widened when she saw the soft white rolls and the pots of jam and marmalade. 'These soft rolls would be good for the old lady,' she thought to herself. 'She would be able to eat them easily instead of trying to suck that hard crusty bread which is all Brigitta can afford.'

Then she turned to Clara and began to tell her again about the old grandmother and her friend, Peter, and the two prettiest goats in all Switzerland.

Clara began to laugh merrily and that morning she seemed able to eat more than she had done for many months.

"My tutor comes this morning," she told Heidi. "We shall have our lessons together. Can you read well, Heidi?"

"I can't read at all," said Heidi. "I've never been to school."

"Well, I couldn't read once," said Clara, "but now I'm twelve and I can read most books. My lessons are really rather boring but they will be more fun with you there — and my tutor will teach you to read."

Heidi's first lesson was disastrous for she did not even know her ABC and the tutor, an earnest young man, did not know where to start. Heidi just could not concentrate, and all the time her thoughts strayed back to her mountain home. She thought of her grandfather — was he missing her? — and Peter and his grandmother, and Little Swan and Little Bear. When, oh when, could she go back to them all?

Heidi grew more and more fond of Clara as the weeks passed. But it was clear to see that she was not happy. She was quite unable to get along with Fraulein Rottenmeier, who simply did not understand Heidi's longing to see the grass and the trees. She thought Heidi was an unruly, mischievous child, and Heidi learnt that she must act in a restrained and quiet way if she was not to be perpetually scolded by the stern housekeeper. Herr Sesemann, Clara's father, however, was a good, generous man, devoted to his invalid daughter, and he wanted Heidi to be happy in her new home. Several times on his visits he tried to question Heidi and find out why she was so quiet and withdrawn.

But Heidi would shake her head and remain silent. How could she tell this stranger her innermost thoughts? He wouldn't understand about the wind in the fir trees and the sweet taste of goat's milk.

One day, Clara's grandmother came to stay at the house while her father was away on another business trip. Heidi liked her the minute she set eyes on her, but once again Fraulein Rottenmeier, who never missed an opportunity to show her dislike of Heidi, told her sharply to keep out of sight until Clara had had time to have a long talk with her grandmother.

Heidi obeyed, going down to the study and sitting in a corner. Soon, however, Sebastian came looking for her. "Come along," he said. "You

are wanted in the drawing-room."

Clara's grandmother had beautiful white hair and the kindest, shrewdest eyes you can imagine. She wore a lovely lacey kind of dress and when Heidi entered the room, she held out her hands to her.

"I saw you when I came in," she said, "but then you vanished."

Heidi smiled and went over to her. She knew how much Clara adored her grandmother and she was ready to love her too.

Soon, the old lady began inviting Heidi to her room. "I have some pretty books," she said. "I will help you to read them."

At first, Heidi shook her head. "I don't know my ABC," she said. "And I can't read anything."

"Then together we shall surprise everyone, including Clara," said the old lady. "I will teach you."

So at last, Heidi began to take an interest in books. The book she loved best had pictures in it of mountains and tall trees that made her think of the fir trees at home. And slowly she began to want to read the words under the pictures.

"As soon as you can read the words," Clara's grandmother told her, "you shall have the book for your very own."

Heidi turned the pages of the wonderful book. On one page there were the mountains and the fresh green grass and the tall trees. And on another page there were pictures of goats. There was even a white one just like Little Swan.

"I will try hard to learn," she said.

But now every time she looked at the pictures, Heidi felt a funny

choked feeling in her throat and sometimes her eyes swam with tears. If only she could go home!

Once she even tried to run away but she was soon lost in the busy streets of the big city. Finally she had had to ask the way back to Clara's house.

She was so severely lectured by Fraulein Rottenmeier that she did not dare to try to run away again. Nor did she like to answer the kindly white-haired lady who had seen her tears. "Why are you so unhappy, Heidi?" she had asked once. "Why do you cry sometimes?"

"I cannot tell you," Heidi had said, fearing that she would hurt the old lady's feelings and receive another scolding from the housekeeper. "I must keep it to myself."

"Then surely you can tell God," said Clara's grandmother. "He knows everything, but He likes to be told. Why don't you, Heidi?"

"I don't know how to pray," said Heidi.

"You don't have to know," said the old lady. "When you speak to God, that's praying. Just tell Him what troubles you. He will listen and make everything happy again for you in His own good time."

That night Heidi told God everything about her longing for the mountains and the fresh air, about Fraulein Rottenmeier's dislike of her and about how she had run away. Finally she begged Him to let her go home to her grandfather.

Clara's grandmother told no one that Heidi was learning to read. Then, one day, as they sat together with Clara, she suddenly said, "Now Heidi will read to us."

Clara gasped with astonishment then began clapping her hands with delight as Heidi took up the book, and began to read the words in her high, clear voice.

"That was lovely, Heidi," said Clara, when the reading was over. And she held out her thin arms to Heidi and kissed her.

The Ghost

AFTER THE old lady had gone, the house seemed sadly empty although Clara had told Heidi that her grandmother had made a particularly long visit.

Heidi missed her almost as much as Clara did. She had been so kind and gentle that she had made Heidi's life a little happier. Now she had gone, Fraulein Rottenmeier seemed even stricter and more forbidding. Heidi grew more and more unhappy. She ate very little and as she got thinner her cheeks lost all their rosy glow.

And then something very strange and mysterious began to happen in the house. Both Sebastian and the maid insisted they had seen a ghost! In the middle of the night, the big front door, which was always heavily bolted, swung open and a pale white figure appeared on the front step.

Even Fraulein Rottenmeier was suddenly overcome with nerves and refused to go into the dark cellar or climb into the attic.

It all seemed so serious that Clara's father was sent for, and he returned home as quickly as he could. Soon, he had been told all about the ghost.

The idea of a ghost in the house was frightening not only to the servants but to the children, and Clara had had several screaming fits which didn't improve her health at all. Heidi, in her unhappiness, hardly seemed to notice the upset in the house.

Herr Sesemann made jokes about the ghost and said he would certainly enjoy meeting it. But the servants were by now so frightened that he saw he must take the matter seriously.

At last, late one night, he sent for the family doctor. Herr Doctor was a grey-haired man with a fresh complexion and two bright, kindly eyes.

He looked somewhat anxious as he entered the house for he thought something must have happened to Clara. Instead, he found her father waiting for him.

"Don't be alarmed, friend," laughed Herr Sesemann. "Clara is all right. I sent for you to help me catch a ghost."

The doctor smiled. "Well, that's the most unusual request I've had in all my life," he said. "Tell me about this ghost of yours."

After he had heard the story, the doctor asked, "Where do we keep watch?"

"In this room that leads off the hall," said Clara's father, taking his arm and leading him into a small room where there were two comfortable armchairs waiting for them. The candles were alight on the table, and there was a bottle of wine and some glasses on the sideboard. It was a cozy place to sit and wait.

The two men were old friends and they talked contentedly together for some time until the grandfather clock in the hall struck one.

"Listen, Sesemann, can you hear something?" the doctor asked suddenly.

As they listened, they clearly heard the noise of the bolt being softly drawn and then the big key being turned in the lock. A draught of cold air told them that the front door was being opened.

Herr Sesemann picked up a revolver and the doctor did likewise.

Then they stepped into the hall. The moon's silvery light was shining in through the open door. And there, in the doorway, stood a white figure.

"Who is it? Who is there?" roared the doctor, advancing on the white figure.

Suddenly it turned and gave a low whimpering cry. There, in her long white nightgown, stood Heidi, her feet bare, staring with wild, frightened eyes at the two men.

"Why, it's Heidi!" exclaimed Herr Sesemann in astonishment.

"Leave her to me," said the doctor, immediately. "I must see to her. She is obviously walking in her sleep." And very gently, he took hold of Heidi's hand and led her upstairs to her bedroom.

Heidi was trembling violently as they reached the room and the doctor gathered her up in his arms and laid her carefully on the bed. He pulled the blanket up to cover her and then he took her hand in his. "Now tell me where you were wanting to go, Heidi," he said softly.

"I didn't want to go anywhere," said Heidi. "I didn't know I was downstairs, I really didn't."

"Were you dreaming?" asked the kindly doctor.

And Heidi said, "Yes, yes, I dream every night and it's always about the same things. I dream I am back with Grandfather and I hear the fir

trees singing outside, and Little Swan and Little Bear are waiting for me in their shed. Then I wake up and I am still here in this big room."

With that she began to weep as if her heart would break. All the tears that she had been holding back for so long came bursting out and her little body was racked with sobs.

"I see," said the doctor. "Yes, I see and I think I understand." And he patted Heidi's little hand. "Cry now, it will do you good. In the morning you will feel better." Then he got up and left the room.

Herr Sesemann was waiting for him in the hall. "What's wrong?" he asked. "Is she sick?"

"She is desperately home-sick," said the doctor. "She is breaking her heart here in Frankfurt and is unusually pale and thin for a child of her age. She must be sent home with all possible speed."

Heidi Returns to the Mountain

IN THE MORNING, Herr Sesemann told the servants that their ghost would no longer trouble the household. Then he sent for Heidi. In a few kind words he told her that, on the good doctor's advice, he was going to send her back to her grandfather.

Speechless with happiness, Heidi could only stand in front of him, her hands at her side. Only her eyes glowed and sparkled like stars in her pale face.

"We must tell Clara," said Herr Sesemann. "And then you must pack your clothes. I mean to send you on your journey today."

Heidi flew to Clara to tell her the wonderful news. But some of her joy left her when she saw her friend's sadness as her eyes filled with tears.

"Don't cry, Clara," she begged. "You will come and visit us up in the mountain, and Grandfather will give you sweet goat's milk and toasted cheese and you will grow strong."

Clara lost some of her sadness as she saw her kind friend's happiness and began to plan what presents she could give her to take back to the people on the mountain.

"You must take at least a dozen soft white rolls, back to the grandmother," she said. "And you can have as many of my dresses as you wish. And Father will give you tobacco for your grandfather. Oh, there are so many things you must take back to the mountains."

By the afternoon, Heidi's big new trunk was packed and Clara gave her a basket for the soft white rolls. Heidi, though dressed in one of the new dresses Clara had given her, insisted on wearing her old battered straw hat so that her grandfather would instantly know her again!

"Why not wear this one with the feather?" Clara pleaded. "It suits you so well, and then when you reach the top of the mountain, you can put on your old straw one." And to please her friend, Heidi at last agreed.

Then Sebastian came to the big front door with the carriage and Herr Sesemann ordered him to take great care of the little girl and see that she was safely delivered into her grandfather's hands. He also gave him a parcel, and a letter for Alm-Uncle which told him all that had happened to Heidi and why she was being sent home.

The ride in the train was fun for Heidi now that she was on her way home and her eyes sparkled. "You don't have to go all the way with me to Dorfli," she told Sebastian, for she guessed he was longing to get back to the city.

Sebastian hesitated. It was true, he loved the city and wasn't really looking forward to the journey out to the mountain village. But he had promised his master he would look after Heidi. Then, as luck would have it, outside Maienfeld Station, he saw a man with a cart. It was the miller from Dorfli.

"Are you going back soon?" he asked, and when the miller nodded, he continued, "would you take this child and her trunk back with you?"

"I would," said the miller, looking curiously at Heidi for he knew her story.

"You can go back on the next train," Heidi said to Sebastian. "The miller will take me to Dorfli and I can make my own way up the mountain. Grandfather will fetch the trunk tomorrow."

Sebastian sighed with relief. He took Heidi aside and gave her a thick rolled parcel and the letter for her grandfather. "Be careful not to lose the parcel," he warned. "It's a present from the master."

"I'll take care of it," Heidi said, putting it in her basket with the letter. "Goodbye, Sebastian, thank you for being so kind to me in Frankfurt," and she held out her hand to him.

As they trundled along the rough road, the miller said very little, but Heidi told him about the rich home she had left and how she had longed to be with her grandfather every minute of the time she had been away.

The miller lifted her down from his cart when they reached the village and, with her basket over her arm, Heidi began climbing up the steep path that led up the mountain — and to her grandfather.

She climbed as fast as she could and when at last she caught sight of the old hut where Peter lived, she was filled with excitement.

Would his grandmother be still alive? Would she still remember the sound of her voice?

Gasping for breath, she began to run, and she burst into the hut like a small whirlwind. The old woman in the corner of the room heard the light steps and cried, "Oh, that sounds just like my little Heidi. If only she could come to see me again!"

"It's me, it's me!" Heidi cried. And she knelt down beside the old woman and took her hand.

Peter's grandmother put out her other hand and stroked Heidi's curly hair, tears trickling down over her wrinkled cheeks.

"Don't cry. I am back for ever," Heidi said. "And I've brought you a present." And she took the rolls from her basket and heaped them into the grandmother's lap.

"They will make you strong again," she cried, "for they're made of soft white bread which is easy to eat."

Then Peter's mother, Brigitta, came in and she was so surprised to see Heidi that she collapsed into a chair. "And how smart you look!" she exclaimed. "The pretty dress and the hat with the feather in it."

Heidi took off her smart new hat and handed it to Brigitta. "Take it," she said. "I would rather wear my own." And she took the battered old straw hat out of her basket and put it on. "Now Grandfather will know me at once," she added.

"You'd better be careful," warned Brigitta, "for since you went away, his temper is a hundred times fiercer. He goes about with a scowl

on his face and when he's in the village, everybody keeps out of his way."

"I must go to him now, at once," Heidi cried, running to the door. "But I will be back tomorrow. Goodbye grandmother, goodbye Brigitta."

As she began climbing the mountain again, Heidi could scarcely breathe for wonder and excitement. It was more beautiful than ever she had remembered it. Already the sun was turning the snow-covered peaks into gleaming gold. And above her head the rosy-pink clouds floated lightly across the sky.

At last she caught sight of the top of the fir trees above the hut roof, and then the roof itself, and at last the whole hut. There was her grandfather sitting on the bench, smoking his pipe, just as she had pictured him so often in her dreams.

Heidi rushed up to him before he saw her coming. She threw her arms around his neck, and whispered, "Grandfather, Grandfather," over and over again. She couldn't say anything else.

The old man said nothing but for the first time for many years, his eyes were wet with tears. Then he took Heidi on to his knee and after looking at her for a moment, he said, "So you have come back to me, Heidi!"

"Yes, yes, Grandfather," Heidi said, laughing and crying, all at the same time. "I'll never, ever leave you again."

Hand in hand, they went indoors and Heidi's eyes flashed around the hut as she looked to see if there were any changes. But the room was just as she had remembered it.

Then, after her grandfather had poured her out a bowl of milk, she gave him the letter and the parcel. The old man read the letter and

nodded once or twice as he began to understand the whole story. Then he undid the parcel and found inside a large amount of money which, Herr Sesemann had written, was all for Heidi.

"But I don't want any money," Heidi exclaimed at once.

"You could buy new dresses and a new bed with it," grandfather said, half teasing her, as he knew how unimportant such things were to Heidi.

But Heidi shook her head and taking up the money, she put it in the bottom of the cupboard. Then she skipped over to the ladder and climbed up into the hay-loft.

Her grandfather heard her cry out in distress, "My bed has gone!"

"We can soon make another one," he called back at once.

Heidi climbed down the ladder and saw that her grandfather was already taking out clean warm covers.

Before she could say any more, there was a shrill whistle. It was Peter with the goats. Out she ran, clapping her hands with pleasure when she saw Little Swan and Little Bear. They seemed to remember her too and ran to her as if it was only yesterday since she had seen them. Heidi hugged them each in turn.

Peter's face was alight with happiness too, at the sight of Heidi, for he had missed her far more than he would ever admit. His days had been long and dreary since she went away.

"I'll come out with you tomorrow," she told him, "if Grandfather will let me."

The next day, Heidi told the old man what she was going to do with the money. "I'm going to buy Peter's grandmother white bread from the village so that she never needs to eat that hard black bread ever again," she said.

And then she got out her wonderful book that Clara's grandmother had given her and, to her grandfather's astonished delight, began to read to him.

Later that day, he took her down the mountain to visit Peter's hut, and for an hour or more she read to the blind woman, in her clear voice. They were wonderful words she chose to read, words about the happiness God brought to those who were faithful to Him and loved Him. And the old woman looked more peaceful than she had done for a very long time.

What a wonderful day it was and the next day, which was Sunday, a very special thing happened. Her grandfather got out his best long coat

with silver buttons, the coat he hadn't worn for longer than he cared to remember, and said he would like to take Heidi down to Dorfli.

"Can we go to church?" Heidi asked.

And the old man nodded.

That was a day never to be forgotten. With Heidi at his side, the old man looked much less forbidding and the villagers began giving him friendly smiles. 'He can't be as bad as everyone says,' they thought, 'or how could the child look so happy and proud as she holds his hand?' So after church, several people came up and spoke to them, and the parson came and shook his hand in front of all the villagers. At last, the old Alm-Uncle began to be accepted into their midst.

The Letter

TOWARDS THE start of the winter, Peter brought a letter with him. He had collected it in the village.

"It's from Clara," Heidi said, full of excitement. "She's coming to see us. Isn't it wonderful? We'll make her strong again, Grandfather! We'll do it between us."

But although Heidi did not know it, Clara was not very well and on the doctor's advice, her journey had to be postponed.

Instead the good doctor himself came to the mountains. He had been very lonely and unhappy in recent months, as his daughter — the only relative he had in the world — had caught a bad fever and died. There seemed almost nothing to live for and Herr Sesemann persuaded him to take a holiday in the mountains to try and forget his grief.

"You must take my presents for me," Clara had said bravely, for she was bitterly disappointed at not being able to go herself. And she showed him the thick warm shawl and the box of little cakes she had bought for the grandmother. Then there was a great long sausage for Peter and all kinds of mysterious packages for Heidi herself, and of course some tobacco for her grandfather.

So the good doctor set out and when the moment came and he found himself climbing the steep path that led to Heidi's home, he wondered what he would say to Heidi. She was expecting Clara and her grandmother and she would surely be bitterly disappointed.

Heidi was disappointed but she was too tender-hearted to show her grief to the good doctor. Besides she never forgot how the doctor had made it possible for her to come home. She hugged him and pulled him into the hut to meet her grandfather.

The two men liked each other on sight and there was so much to talk about, so many questions to ask and be answered that Heidi's eyes soon began to sparkle with happiness.

The big parcel was brought up the next day, and Heidi could scarcely wait to run down the mountain with the box of little cakes and the wonderful soft warm shawl. The big meat sausage made Peter's eyes grow wide with longing — it was ages since he had had anything so delicious to eat — and all to himself!

The old woman in her corner wept with happiness as Heidi put the shawl round her thin, bent shoulders, and Brigitta said, "What an angel you are, Heidi! It's just as if the sun was always shining in this dark room when you are here."

The days that followed did much to restore the doctor's happiness and faith in life. Heidi showed him all her special places on the mountain, and Alm-Uncle talked to him about the flowers and trees and the health-giving herbs that grew wild near their home.

There was so much to see and do that the days passed all too quickly and he could scarcely believe it when the day came for him to return to Frankfurt.

"Clara will come to see you in the summer," he promised, as Heidi clung to him, "with her grandmother! She will have a happy time here, I know, and just think of all the things I have to tell her when I get back."

"And will you come again?" asked Heidi, who had grown more and more fond of the doctor.

"I will," he said, "I will, Heidi," for he had found peace and happiness in the mountains and he loved this child as he had his own daughter.

Heidi's Winter Home

THE SNOW was lying so high all round the hut that it was almost level with the windows.

"I have decided that we must spend the winter in Dorfli," said her grandfather. "There's a tumble-down house which I can make snug and warm for us both. And you can go to school."

Heidi was thrilled. She had secretly longed to go to school so that she could have more books to read. And more than anything, she wanted her grandfather to be completely accepted by the villagers.

The very next day, they packed up all their belongings, and shutting the mountain hut they set out for Dorfli with Little Swan and Little Bear. The house was big and rambling with high ceilings and shutters that let in the wind. But soon grandfather was busy with his saw and hammer and by the end of the day, it began to feel cozy.

Outside, he made a shed for his two goats and Heidi spent some time
with them so they would not feel home-sick.

All through the winter, Heidi went to school and the villagers grew
friendlier and friendlier. Grandfather was a familiar figure round Dorfli
now, in the shops and at church on Sundays and soon everyone had
forgotten all the terrible things that used to be told about him. Everyone

had a friendly word for him, and he in turn was always ready to help people.

Peter came often to the old house, particularly when he learnt that grandfather would always give him a good meal. Heidi was anxious that he should learn to read properly and bullied him into taking out his school books and going over his lessons. His teacher had almost given him up and never asked him to read aloud in class. But one day, to the astonishment of everybody, he stood up and read from his exercise book. That was one of the most important moments in his life, and Heidi was just as pleased as he was at the impression he made. The teacher just couldn't believe his ears!

All through the winter Clara wrote long letters to Heidi and one day, when the winter was over and the spring sunshine was melting the snow on the mountain, Heidi got a very exciting letter. 'At last!' Clara wrote, 'the good doctor says I am strong enough to make the journey this Spring. He talks endlessly of his holiday with you and I am so looking forward to seeing you again.'

Heidi was so excited. She rushed to tell her grandfather. "We must go back to our home on the mountain," she said, "and get everything ready for Clara!"

"We can return tomorrow," said her grandfather, smiling at Heidi's excitement. "Don't worry, we shall have everything ready for your friend before she arrives."

How lovely it was to be back home! The goats jumped in the air on their thin legs, bleating for joy. And Heidi ran in and out of the hut as wildly happy as they were to be back.

Early one morning, Peter brought another letter from Clara. She wrote that she was now beginning to prepare for the journey. It would not be long before they saw each other again.

But it was nearly the end of June before Clara came at last. Heidi was

just turning the corner of the hut when she saw the procession coming up the mountain. And she gave such a loud cry that her grandfather came running out of the shed to see if anything was wrong.

"Look! Look!" Heidi cried, pointing down the mountain.

The old man saw a strange sight. Up the mountain came two men carrying a sedan chair in which sat a girl wrapped in shawls, and following behind on a white horse, came an old lady with a straight back. Behind her came another man pushing a wheelchair.

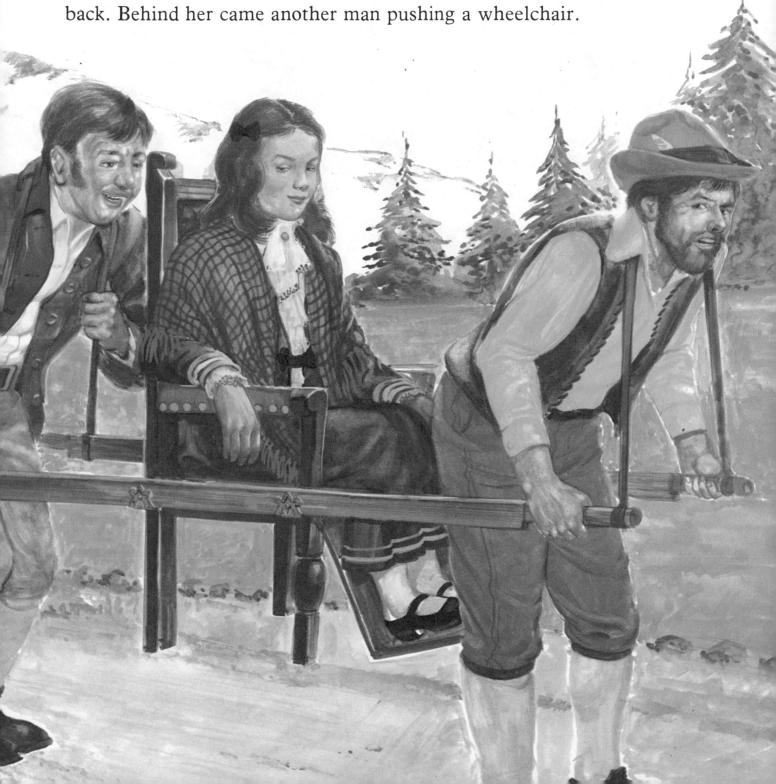

Heidi began jumping for joy as the procession drew nearer and nearer. At last it arrived at the hut. Clara was lifted into the wheelchair and Heidi was able to welcome her properly to the mountain.

Clara's thin white face was beginning to look rosy with the fresh mountain air and her grandmother smiled with happiness, as she grasped the old man's hand in hers.

"I had thought to take her back to Dorfli," she said. "But now I am beginning to wonder if I might not leave her with you."

"We'll take good care of her," said the old man. "The pure mountain air will soon bring the roses to her cheeks."

So it was settled and the old man carried Clara into the hut. Her grandmother, with her arm round Heidi, followed.

What wonderful days they were for Clara! Never in all her life had she known such freedom. It is true she could not walk but Heidi and her grandfather were always there to push her farther up the mountainside, so that she could see the carpets of wild flowers and listen to the wind among the trees. Her bed was in the hay-loft next to Heidi where the old man, as tender as a woman, laid her each night.

Peter was jealous of Heidi's new friend, but he said very little when Heidi insisted that he should help her to push Clara's chair. He became quiet and surly and would stay apart from the girls, muttering or cutting the air angrily with his stick.

One never-to-be-forgotten day, as Heidi sat with Clara under a tree, the goats grazing nearby and Peter watching them, the girl vowed that she felt strong enough to put her feet to the ground.

"You must lean on me," said Heidi, breathless with excitement. "We could take just a few little steps together."

"Peter," she called, "come and help." Peter did not want to, but there was something about the way Heidi spoke to him that made him do what she said.

They supported Clara between them, and very gingerly she rose out of her chair. Then slowly she put one foot forward and then the other so that she was taking proper steps. She only managed a tiny walk before she sank back into the chair. But that was enough!

And that was the beginning of Clara's slow recovery. Gradually, with Alm-Uncle's help, she began to walk, leaning on his strong arm. Clara's grandmother, knowing that her grandchild was in good hands, had gone to visit a friend in a nearby town.

The girls wrote to her faithfully but not a word did they say about Clara's walking.

"It must be a surprise," said Heidi. "A wonderful, wonderful surprise!"

A Happy Ending

EVER HAD the mountain known such a fine summer and Clara's face grew sun-tanned and round, as every day she found herself able to walk a little farther, though never without Alm-Uncle's strong arm to lean on.

Sometimes, Heidi left her to go down the mountain to visit the old woman and read to her, for never would she desert her friends. And she saw to it that the old lady always had delicious soft white bread to eat.

On these days when Heidi left Clara at the hut, after Peter had brought back the goats, Alm-Uncle would give Clara salt to feed them with, and the two goats licked her hands and gambolled round her as if they had known her all their lives.

One morning, towards the end of that wonderful summer, Clara's grandmother came riding up the mountain on her white horse and with her came two men carrying an enormous package for Heidi.

When she saw Clara sitting on the bench with Heidi beside her, she cried, "What's this? Where is your wheelchair?"

And then suddenly the two children rose to their feet and began slowly to walk towards her, Clara's hand on Heidi's shoulder.

The old lady was speechless with astonishment. Then Clara, rosy-cheeked, was in her arms, spilling out the wonderful news that she could walk.

Her grandmother's eyes filled with tears of joy as she turned to Alm-Uncle and took his big hand in hers. "I must send a telegram at once to her father," she said at last. "He must come here and see this miracle for himself. Nothing I could say could ever thank you, my dear Alm-Uncle."

Two days later, Herr Sesemann himself arrived at the hut. As he reached the door, two figures came towards him. One, a tall girl with brown hair and pink cheeks, leaning on Heidi, whose eyes were alight with happiness.

"Don't you know me, Papa?" Clara said. Unable to believe what he saw, her father ran to her and clasped her in his arms.

He could not find words to express his joy at the sight of his daughter, able to walk and looking so well and strong. Then Clara's grandmother came out of the hut and with her was Alm-Uncle. The two men shook hands warmly, and went into the hut talking in low voices.

At last, after they had all had a drink of goat's milk and eaten some of grandfather's bread and toasted cheese, Herr Sesemann said, "I owe everything to you, Alm-Uncle, and to Heidi here. What can I do for you in return?"

Alm-Uncle coughed a little and said, "My friend, let us go outside for a short stroll." When they were out of earshot of the hut, he said, "I am growing old. I have nothing to leave the child when I am gone. If you could promise me that Heidi shall never have to go and live among strangers, then you will reward me richly for what I have been able to do for Clara."

"I look upon Heidi as a second daughter," said Herr Sesemann warmly. "I give you my solemn word that I will see she has enough to make her independent. She can stay in the mountain for as long as she likes, but our home shall always be hers should she ever need it."

The old man's face lit up with happiness at these words. He puffed at his pipe, secure in the knowledge that Heidi would always be happy. Then Herr Sesemann went on, "But I have news for you. The good doctor has lost his heart to little Heidi. Frankfurt holds little joy for him now and he is making plans to come and settle in Dorfli. He had an idea that you and she might be willing to share the old house you told him about — at least in the winter." Alm-Uncle agreed readily. He enjoyed the doctor's company and it was good to have someone to talk to.

So it was all settled and when the time came to leave the mountain, Alm-Uncle wrapped Clara warmly in her shawls and picked her up in his strong arms.

"I will carry you down the mountainside myself," he said. And her father nodded, knowing that she could not be in safer hands.

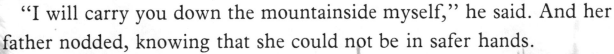

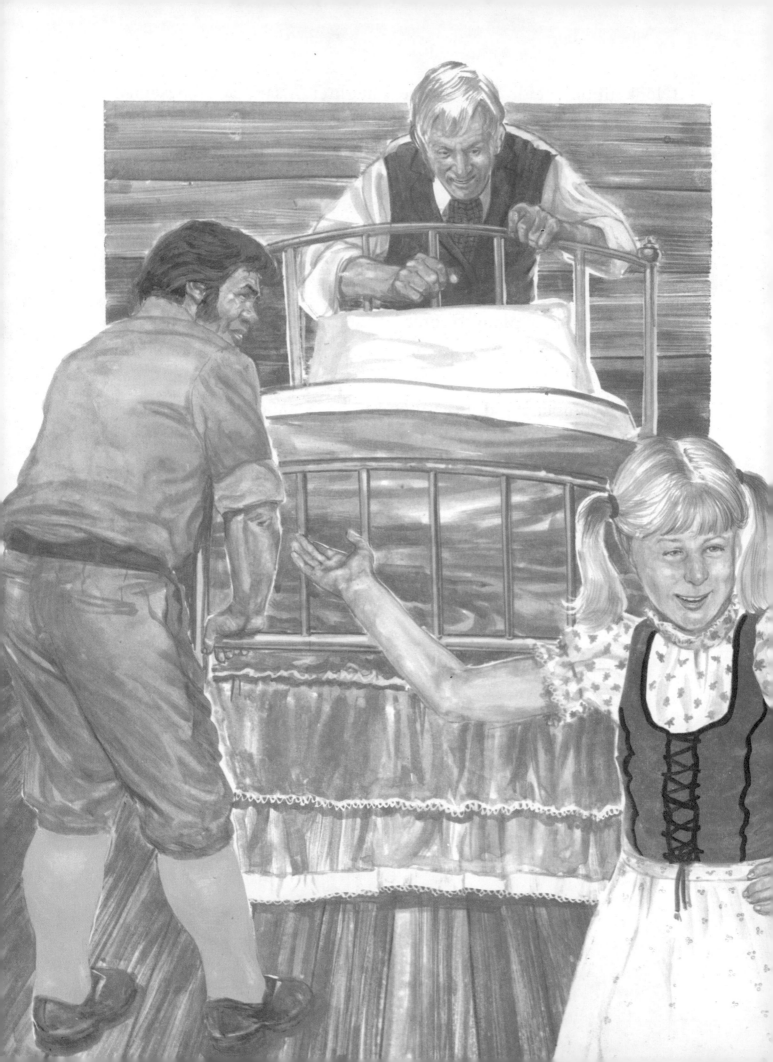